THE
JUNGLE
BOOK

Ladybird Books

Mowgli had lived in the jungle
all his life, and he loved it.

There were all sorts of exciting things to do.
He could swing from tree to tree...

...or play games with his jungle friends.

And there was a wise, wise panther, Bagheera. He taught Mowgli all the laws of the jungle – and the dangers.

But Mowgli never worried about the dangers. Especially when he was with his friend, Baloo.

Mowgli liked to sit on Baloo's large, round tummy...

...and listen to his stories.

And Baloo showed Mowgli where
to find the most delicious bananas.

Sometimes Baloo and Mowgli
would cool off in the river.
Baloo made a wonderful boat!

All the same, there *were* dangers in the jungle. Once, some wicked monkeys captured Mowgli. Luckily, Bagheera and Baloo managed to rescue him.

Then Mowgli met another ugly
customer – Kaa, the python.

Mowgli was so frightened he couldn't move. The great snake opened his mouth wide to swallow him...

...but Bagheera was there again. He gave the snake one terrible blow of his mighty paw, and Kaa slid silently away.

Bagheera made Mowgli promise to be
more careful. And Mowgli kept his
promise – as all little boys should.

Ladybird books are widely available, but in case of difficulty may be ordered by post or telephone from:
Ladybird Books – Cash Sales Department Littlegate Road Paignton Devon TQ3 3BE Telephone 0803 554761

A catalogue record for this book is available from the British Library

Published by Ladybird Books Ltd Loughborough Leicestershire UK
LADYBIRD and the device of a Ladybird are trademarks of Ladybird Books Ltd